THE MARBLE CRUSHER
AND OTHER STORIES

THE MARBLE CRUSHER
AND OTHER STORIES

MICHAEL MORPURGO

ILLUSTRATED BY ALASDAIR BRIGHT

EGMONT

First published in Great Britain as three separate volumes:

The Marble Crusher published 1992
by William Heinemann Ltd
Text copyright © 1992 Michael Morpurgo

Colly's Barn published 1991
by William Heinemann Ltd
Text copyright © 1991 Michael Morpurgo

Conker published 1987
by William Heinemann Ltd
Text copyright © 1987 Michael Morpurgo

This omnibus edition first published 1994
by Mammoth
Reissued 2002 by
Egmont Books Limited
239 Kensington High Street, London W8 6SA

Cover illustration copyright © 2002 Jarrel Akib
Inside illustration copyright © 2002 Alasdair Bright

The moral rights of the author and illustrators have been asserted

ISBN 1 4052 0187 8

10 9 8 7 6 5 4 3 2 1

A CIP catalogue record for this title is available from the British Library

Typeset by Avon DataSet Ltd, Bidford on Avon, Warwickshire
Printed and bound in Great Britain by Cox & Wyman Ltd, Reading,
Berkshire

CONTENTS

THE MARBLE CRUSHER
CHAPTER ONE

ALBERT WAS TEN YEARS OLD. HE WAS A quiet, gentle sort of a boy with a thatch of stiff hair that he twiddled when he was nervous.

He had moved to town from the country-side. 'We have to go where the work is,' his mother had told him, and there was work in the town.

So Albert came from his little village school to a new school, a school which was noisy and full of strange faces. The other children called him Bert, or Herbert, neither of which was his name. They kept asking him questions and they wouldn't leave him alone.

There was somewhere to get away from it all, behind the bike shed in the playground, but never for long. By the end of each day Albert felt like a sponge squeezed dry. He smiled so much that it hurt. He tried to laugh at everyone's jokes, and he believed everything they told him. He was naturally a trusting child, and now, in the first weeks of his new school, he wanted to please everyone, to make friends.

They teased Albert of course, and he was easy enough to tease, but Albert just smiled through it all. They called him 'Twiddler!' and Albert smiled and went on twiddling his hair. He did not seem to mind.

It was Sid Creedy who discovered that Albert would believe almost anything he told him. They were playing football in the playground in break when Sid turned to his friends and said, 'Watch this.' He dribbled the ball over towards Albert, and his friends followed him.

'My dad,' said Sid, 'he played centre-forward for Liverpool. Did for years. Then they asked him to play for England, but he didn't want to – he didn't like the colour of the shirt.'

CHAPTER TWO

THAT EVENING ALBERT TOLD HIS MOTHER all about Sid Creedy's father, but his mother wasn't listening, she was too busy washing up.

Encouraged by his success, Sid Creedy's stories became more and more fantastic. 'You know Mr Cooper, Bert?'

'You mean the PE master?'

'Yes, that's him.' Sid spoke in a confidential whisper, his arm around Albert's shoulder. 'Well, Bert, no one else knows this, but Mr Cooper isn't really a teacher at all – he's an escaped monk.'

'How do you know that, Sid?' said Albert.

'You look at his head,' said Sid. 'It's all bald in the middle isn't it? You know, like Friar Tuck. Anyway I found his brown cloak in the boot of his car. He always wears sandals, and he never swears. And haven't you noticed he sings louder than anyone else in Assembly?'

'But why did he escape?' said Albert.

Sid shrugged his shoulders. 'Didn't like the food,' he said.

'And he knows you know?'

'Course he does, but I told him I'd keep it quiet. You're the only one I've ever told, Bert.'

Albert went home and told his mother, but his mother was busy making his tea.

'Mum,' he said, 'that Mr Cooper at school, he's an escaped monk.'

'Yes dear,' she said. 'Now get those wet shoes off before you catch your death.'

CHAPTER THREE

BACK AT SCHOOL SID CREEDY TOLD ALBERT more and more of his secrets. Every teacher at school it seemed had a deep, dark secret – even the Headmaster, Mr Manners.

'He's got six wives,' said Sid one day, 'like Henry the Eighth.'

'He hasn't!' said Albert.

'Oh yes he has,' said Sid. 'And that Mrs Manners that teaches the Infants, she's just one out of the six. And he's got twenty-two children.'

'He hasn't!' said Albert.

'Oh yes he has,' said Sid, 'and there's two more on the way.'

Back in the classroom, as Sid told his friends, he was triumphant. Albert had swallowed it hook, line and sinker.

At home, Albert tried to tell his mother about Mr Manners. 'Honest, Mum, he's got six wives,' he said with his mouth full of toast.

'What's that dear?'

'Mr Manners, Mum. He's got twenty-two children as well,' said Albert, 'like Henry the Eighth. And he was away from school today.'

'Well, I hope it gets better,' said his mother. And that was that.

CHAPTER FOUR

CONKERS WERE OVER AND IT WAS THE marble season in mid-November. Now Mr Manners hated marbles.

'Treacherous things, marbles,' he said in Assembly one morning. 'Slip on one and you can break a leg, just like that. In the playground, yes, play with them all you wish, but inside my school there will be no marbles. If I see, or so much as smell a marble inside my school, it will be confiscated. And you know what that means.'

'What does that mean, Sid?' Albert asked after Assembly.

'What does what mean?'

'Con . . . confiscated. What does it mean?'

Sid smiled inside himself. 'Crushed,' he said. 'Crushed, that's what it means.'

'Crushed?'

'Same every year,' said Sid, and he turned to his friends. 'Isn't that right, lads?' And they all nodded and turned away to hide their smiles.

Sid went on in a hushed voice. 'It's like this, Bert. If your marbles are confiscated by old Manners, that means he takes them away and puts them through his machine – a marble crusher.'

'A marble crusher?'

'A marble crusher. He keeps it in his room under his desk. I've seen it. We've all seen it. And that's where they all go.'

CHAPTER FIVE

BACK AT HOME ALBERT HAD HIS OWN collection of marbles, but they were no ordinary marbles. They were silver ball-bearings. He had seventy-five of them now, pea size to conker size. They were all lined up on the mantelpiece above his bed. Everyone at school had glass marbles but no one else had silver ball-bearings. Albert was very proud of them.

Over half-term Albert polished them till they shone, and the day school began again he took six of the big ones with him into school. They were cold and heavy in his pocket. And what a sensation they created!

Albert was very good at marbles, and he knew he was particularly good with his silver ones. Over rough ground they kept to a truer line than the glass ones that often bounced off course. So by lunchtime he had won ten marbles. One of them was a blood red, a lovely deep red marble, highly prized because there was a white mist gliding around inside it. Of course everyone wanted to play Albert to try and win one of his silver marbles, but Albert chose the rough ground and he outplayed them all.

It was in reading time, after lunch, that Sid Creedy challenged him to play marbles, but *inside* the classroom. Albert didn't really want to. He preferred the long distances and the potholes of the playground. But he did not want to upset his friend and so he agreed. In the excitement of the game he quite forgot Mr Manners' rule about playing marbles inside the school.

Even on the smooth floor in amongst the chair legs Albert went on winning. He was crouching under the teacher's table, taking careful aim, when Mr Manners came in behind him silently.

'Albert,' he said. 'Albert, are you playing marbles?'

'Oh . . . yes sir,' and Albert remembered at once – he remembered the punishment too and he began to twiddle his hair.

'They will all have to go, all of them mind,' said Mr Manners. 'Empty your pockets, lad,' and he held out his big chalky hand. 'I'm surprised at you, Albert, and disappointed – very disappointed.'

Albert took them out of his pocket one by one and dropped them into Mr Manners' hand. His winnings went first – the blood red too – and then last of all his six great heavy silver ball-bearings. It was as if his blood was being taken from him. The fist closed before his eyes and his marbles were gone.

'A pity, Albert,' Mr Manners said, shaking his head. 'A terrible pity. Lovely marbles too. But you were warned. And we cannot have people breaking school rules can we now?'

'No sir,' said Albert, wondering how long it would be before his marbles went through the crusher, how much longer they had to live.

'Hard luck,' said Sid, when Mr Manners had

gone out. 'You can only just hear the machine, Bert,' he went on. 'It's all modern and silent.'

'You mean the marble crusher?' said Albert, blinking back his tears.

Sid nodded. 'I'm afraid so. They're gonners, Bert. Ten minutes and they'll be so much dust. It's Japanese, very efficient.'

CHAPTER SIX

ALBERT WENT HOME THAT AFTERNOON miserable. He could not bear to think of his beautiful silver marbles being ground down to dust. He was crying bitter tears by the time he reached his front door. He cried up against his mother's apron, and in between the heaving and the snivelling his mother heard the whole story of Mr Manners' terrible machine, how it was unfair, how he would never see his six silver marbles again, nor the blood red, how he hated Mr Manners, all the teachers and everyone at the school, including the dinner ladies.

This time Albert's mother had to listen. She was inside the school gates within five minutes, still in her apron, dragging Albert along by his hand. Albert did not want to go. He did not want her to make a fuss. He did not want to be hauled red-eyed and snivelling through the school gates. Albert's mother never even knocked on the staffroom door. She burst into the room, her eyes searching out the Headmaster.

Mr Manners was halfway to his mouth with a cup of tea, and the other teachers sat around him not knowing quite where to look.

'Mr Manners,' she stormed, 'I sent my son to your school because I thought you would look after him and care for him. And what happens? Albert tells me you have taken away his collection of marbles and you have destroyed them with some horrible machine – Albert calls it "a marble crusher" or some such thing. Never in all my days have I heard of such cruel goings on inside a school. I'm telling you, the authorities are going to hear about this. You haven't heard the last of this, Mr Manners. If this is how teachers treat children these days . . .' And so on and so on.

Mr Manners had put down his teacup and was holding up his hand, much in the same way a policeman might try and stop traffic. 'I think there has been some misunderstanding,' he said. 'Certainly I confiscated Albert's marbles . . .'

'Confiscated! Confiscated! You crushed them Mr Manners, not confiscated them.'

Mr Manners frowned. 'Did Albert tell you that?' And Mr Manners looked down at Albert. Albert was completely bewildered. Never had he seen his mother this angry. He twiddled his hair furiously until his mother slapped his hand away.

'That's what Albert told me,' she said, 'and my son's no liar, Mr Manners. He wouldn't invent such things, he's not like that.'

'Oh, I know that,' said Mr Manners, and he turned to Albert. 'Now tell me, Albert, who told you about this machine, this marble crusher?'

'It was Sid, sir,' said Albert, 'Sid Creedy. He said you've got a great big marble crusher under your desk. He said all the marbles you take away are crushed down to dust. Japanese he said, and very efficient.'

Mr Manners was nodding and he was smiling too. 'And what else does he say, Albert?'

Slowly, very slowly, the truth was beginning to dawn. Albert was beginning to understand. The teachers around were all smiling. He knew Sid Creedy had been lying to him and he wanted his own back.

'He said you've got six wives, sir, like Henry the Eighth, sir; and you've got twenty-two children and there's two more on the way. And he said that Mr Cooper's an escaped monk.'

'Mr Cooper,' said Mr Manners, 'tell me, are you an escaped monk?'

Mr Cooper smiled down at Albert and ruffled his hair. 'No,' he said. 'I've never been a monk, and the way I feel about Sidney Creedy just now I don't think I'd ever qualify. But Mr Manners, what about you? We've only ever met one of your wives and two of your twenty-two children. Where do you keep the others?'

So the whole web of lies was unravelled in front of him. Albert saw his mother laughing with them and he felt ashamed of himself and his stupidity. But Mr Manners put a comforting arm around him.

'Never you mind, Albert,' he said. 'It seems to me you have a nice trusting nature, and it also seems to me that I shall have to teach Master Sidney Creedy a little lesson.'

CHAPTER SEVEN

NEXT MORNING, AFTER ASSEMBLY, MR Manners made them all sit down in the School Hall. He had something to say, something very important he said. He put his hands on his hips and cleared his throat.

'Teachers can be wrong, children,' he began, 'like anyone else they can be wrong from time to time. And I was wrong to confiscate Albert's marbles yesterday. You see, in the heat of the moment I quite forgot that it takes two to play marbles, doesn't it? Now I can't remember, so I'm going to have to ask whoever it was playing marbles with Albert yesterday to stand up.'

Albert looked down at the floor and twiddled his hair. Everyone else looked at Sid Creedy so he had to stand up.

'Sid Creedy,' said Mr Manners nodding slowly. 'Well, Sid, it seems only fair then that I also confiscate your marbles. I think that's only right, don't you?' Sid said nothing. 'You'd better come up here, Sid,' said Mr Manners;

and reluctantly Sid poured a bagful of marbles into Mr Manner's hand.

'Nice ones,' said Mr Manners examining them closely. 'What a pity, what a terrible pity,' And then he went out. Sid Creedy came back and sat down next to Albert.

'Will he put them in the marble crusher?' Albert whispered.

'Don't be silly, Bert.' Sid Creedy was irritated. 'Course not, you dumb Herbert, there's no such thing as a marble crusher. I was having you on wasn't I? You'd believe anything wouldn't you?'

From down the corridor came a distant electrical hum like a muffled power drill. It lasted for a few seconds and then there was a long silence. They heard the staffroom door slam and then Mr Manners' crisp footsteps coming back towards the School Hall.

'There,' he said as he shut the door behind

him. 'That's that then.' He was holding two paper bags. One he gave to Albert and one to Sid Creedy. 'They've been through the marble crusher,' he said. 'Just like sand now, colourful sand.'

And he spoke now to the whole school. 'Well children,' he said. 'You can see now that you would be well advised *never* to play marbles inside my school again. If you do it will merely mean more work for my marble crusher. It's Japanese you know. Very efficient!'

COLLY'S BARN
CHAPTER ONE

SOMEONE HAD TO CLEAN OUT THE OLD barn. Grandad had a bad knee and her mother and father were busy, so Annie had to do it all by herself. But she wasn't alone. You were never quite alone in the old barn.

Screecher, the barn owl, looked down at her from his perch on the beam above her. She knew that the swallows would be watching her from their nests high on the roof joists. But the owls and the swallows were as much a part of the barn as the mud walls and the thatched roof and she paid them no attention.

It was hot work and smelly too, but Annie was used to that. After all she had grown up on a farm and on a farm there were always smells of one kind or another. This was no worse than most.

'Be nice if the cows would learn to clean up after themselves,' said Grandad from the door of the barn. 'I thought maybe you could do with some water.' They sat down side by side on a hay bale. Annie drank till the bottle was empty. Grandad was looking around him. 'This barn, your father wants to knock it down, you know,' he said.

'What for?' said Annie.

'Old fashioned, he says, and maybe he's right.' Grandad prodded the wall with his stick. 'Cob that is, just mud, a few stones, straw; and it's lasted all that time. Course there's a few cracks in it here and there, but I told your father, it'll go on for a few years yet.'

On the beam above them Screecher stretched his legs and flexed his talons. Grandad looked up. 'And Screecher, he's been here since the place was built, or his family has. Always nest in the same place they do. Same as those swallows, they've been coming here ever since I can remember.' Grandad stood up and leaned on his stick. 'Makes you think,' he said, 'thousands of miles they come every year, across African deserts, over the sea, and straight back to this barn. There's one now.' As he spoke Colly flew in over his head and up to the nest above, fluttered there for a moment and then swooped down again and out of the door.

'Look,' said Annie, 'there's a baby in the nest, you can see its head.'

'So you can,' said Grandad. 'You can hear it too. I wonder what it's saying.'

Annie laughed. 'Birds don't talk,' she said.

'Not like you maybe,' Grandad said, 'and not like me, but they talk all right. We just don't understand what they're saying, that's all. I wonder if they understand us?'

'Course not,' said Annie, but it gave her a lot to think about while she mucked out and when you've got something to think about time passes quickly. She never even noticed the evening coming on and she never once looked up at the swallows nest again. If she had, she'd have seen the fledgling swallow perched precariously on the edge of its nest trying out its wings.

Screecher saw it but did not say anything. Colly was a good mother. She did not need any advice from him as to how to bring up her family. She was his friend too, his oldest friend. They'd been living in the barn longer than any of the other birds. All winter, every winter, he would look forward to the day when Colly would come flying back into the barn, bringing the spring with her. And when she arrived she never rested, not for a moment. She'd be building her nest, working every hour of the daylight. She'd hatch out her eggs and then she'd be flying in and out, in and out, keeping

her family fed, and this year she'd had to feed them all on her own. No one really knew what had happened to her mate. He just went off hunting one morning and never came back. It could have been a car; it could have been a cat.

Screecher was just thinking about the cat when he heard her, and then he saw her creeping in through the door. Everyone warned everyone else. 'Look out! Look out!' they cried as the cat stalked stiffly past the hay bale and sat down under Colly's nest, her tail whisking to and fro, her eyes fixed on the nest above her.

Screecher knew what would happen, he'd seen it all too often before. Suddenly terrified, Colly's last fledgling beat his wings frantically. Then he overbalanced and fell. The cat watched as he fluttered helplessly down towards the floor of the barn. She knew she had only to wait. There was no hurry, no hurry at all. She wasn't even hungry, she'd already had a nest of mice that day. This bird was for playing with.

At that moment Colly came gliding in, a mayfly in her beak. She dived at once, screaming at the cat, banked steeply and came in again. The cat ducked as Colly flashed by and she swiped the air with an unsheathed claw as she passed overhead. The fledgling was flapping his way to the corner of the barn. The cat crawled after him, belly on the ground, ignoring Colly's desperate attempts to drive her off.

There was only one thing Colly could do now. She landed between the cat and her stranded fledgling and hopped away on a leg and a wing pretending to be wounded. 'I've broken it,' she cried. 'I've broken my wing.' The cat stopped, turned and followed her. A big bird was always better sport than a small bird.

Screecher sprang off his perch and floated down on silent wings. The cat heard the whisper of wind through Screecher's feathers and looked up. She saw the spread of white wings and the talons coming at her, open and deadly. She backed away in surprise. Screecher had never challenged her before.

'Colly,' said Screecher, keeping his eyes on the cat as she slunk away. 'I'm going to pick him up and put him back in the nest. Tell him to hold still. Tell him not to be frightened.'

His talons curled carefully under and around the fledgling. Then he took off, lifting

him higher and higher until at last he was hovering above the nest and could let him go. The fledgling dropped down into the nest and huddled, complaining, in a corner. Colly landed beside him. 'I told you you weren't ready to fly yet, didn't I? I told him, Screecher. Wait till your wings are stronger, I said. Wait till tomorrow. But they don't listen.'

Screecher shivered. 'I think there's a storm coming,' he said. 'I can feel it in the wind. I'd best be off hunting before the rain comes,' and he opened his wings and lifted off the beam.

'Screecher,' Colly called after him. 'Thanks a million. I won't forget it, not ever.'

'What are friends for,' said Screecher as he floated away out through the barn door and into the dusk.

The road was always the best hunting ground. The hedgerows on either side were full of rustling voles and mice and rats. He had a good night of it. Five kills he made, but his two scrawny owlets just ate and asked for more. The rumble of thunder was coming dangerously close now. He'd been caught out in a storm once before. Once was enough. 'I'm telling you, you can't go hunting with wet feathers,' he told them, but that didn't stop them from grumbling on about how hungry they were.

CHAPTER TWO

ALL NIGHT, AS THE STORM RAGED OUTSIDE, the birds in the barn huddled together in their nests, burying their heads in each other to blot out the sound of the thunder. The wind whined and whistled through the eaves, the walls shuddered and the beams creaked and groaned. But Screecher and Colly were not worried. They'd been through storms like this before and the old barn had held together.

Screecher thought the worst of it was over. He was peering through a crack in the wall, looking for the first light of dawn on the distant

hills, when the lightning struck. In one blinding flash night was turned into day. A deafening clap of thunder shook the barn and a fireball glowing orange and blue rolled around the barn and disappeared through the door. Through the smoke Screecher could see that the crack in the wall was suddenly a gaping hole and above him the roof was open to the rain.

Grandad's bad knee kept him in bed the next morning and Annie was at school when her father and mother discovered the hole in the barn wall.

'Lucky it didn't catch fire,' said Annie's mother.

'Might have been better if it had,' said her father. 'One way or another that barn's got to come down now. I've been saying it for years.'

'You could patch it up,' Annie's mother replied.

Her father shook his head. 'Waste of time and money. New modern shed, that's what we need. I'll have a bulldozer in, we'll soon have it down.'

'Grandad won't like it,' she said. 'You know how much he likes the old buildings. I don't want you upsetting him again.'

'It's just a tumbled down old barn,' he said. 'Anyway, Grandad won't know till it's all over. He won't be out of bed for a couple of days, not with his knee like it is. And not a word to Annie, she tells him everything. Thick as thieves they are, those two.'

    High above them
in the old barn, Screecher
and Colly were perched side by
side listening to every word. 'What'll we
do?' said Screecher. 'There's nowhere else to
nest for miles around; and even if there was my
two children won't be ready to fly for another
month or more. I can't move them and I won't
leave them. I won't.'

Colly said nothing. She flew off to join the swifts and housemartins as they skimmed low over the high grass in Long Meadow. The message that Screecher and his family were in trouble soon got around. At first some of them refused to help. There was a rumour that Screecher had killed a cock robin not so long ago. The sparrows and the crows, and there were a lot of them, said that it was nothing to do with them, that everyone had to look after themselves. But all the birds that lived in the barn, the fan-tailed doves, the swallows, the swifts, and the little wren, needed no persuading. After all they'd seen Screecher, only the day before, diving down to rescue Colly's fledgling from the cat.

'I've got babies in my nest just like Screecher,' said the wren. 'And anyway, if they knock down the barn where are we going to nest next year and the year after that?'

All day long the birds argued, and it was almost dark before they were all agreed at last. 'Then we'll start work at first light tomorrow,' said Colly. 'Let's all get some sleep.'

CHAPTER THREE

THE NEXT MORNING GRANDAD LOOKED OUT from his bedroom window at the crowd of birds swirling around the bar. 'They must be after the flies in the thatch,' he said to Annie's mother when she brought him his early morning tea.

'Who knows,' she said. 'You just stay in bed and rest that knee of yours.'

Annie sat down to breakfast in the kitchen. 'There's swarms of birds out there,' she said. 'Like bees. What're they up to?'

'Who knows,' said her father. 'Eat up, you'll be late for school.'

As she got off the school bus that afternoon Annie could see the birds still soaring and swooping around the barn. She ran up the lane to get a closer look. Grandad was there in his dressing-gown. 'I wouldn't have thought it possible,' he said. 'You see that hole in the wall? Must have happened in the storm. They're mending it, that's what they're doing.'

As Annie watched she saw the swifts and swallows and housemartins come flying in with mud in their beaks.They fluttered briefly at the wall and flew off again. The crows and buzzards hovered over the roof before landing

with their twigs and straw, and the wren darted
to and fro, her beak full of
moss and lichen. 'Your
father's not going
to believe this,'
said Grandad.

And he was right. He didn't. Nor did her
mother. They wouldn't even come out to look.
'You'll catch your death, Grandad,' Annie's
mother said. 'Back to bed with you now.'

Annie tried to tell them but they wouldn't
listen to her either. They didn't want
to hear another word
about the barn
or the birds,
not one word.

'You'll tire yourself out, Colly,' said Screecher that night.

'Don't you worry,' Colly said. 'These wings have taken me to Africa and back five times now, they'll carry me a lot further yet. A few more days and the barn will be as good as new again and then they won't need to knock it down, will they?'

'We need more help with the roof,' said Screecher. 'I'll fly down to the river tomorrow and ask the herons. They're the experts.' But Colly didn't even hear him, she was fast asleep.

CHAPTER FOUR

ANNIE WANTED TO BE QUITE SURE Grandad was right, so all weekend she stayed and she watched the birds flying back and forth. Even Screecher was out flying by day and she'd never seen that before. He was fetching and carrying just like all the others. Of all of them though, it was the swallows, and one of them in particular, that worked hardest, swooping down to the muddy puddles and up to the barn wall with never a pause for rest. Annie knew now for certain that Grandad had not been imagining things.

'It's true,' she said. 'What Grandad says, it's all true.' But they still wouldn't believe her. When she shouted at them she was sent off to bed early. Grandad came to comfort her. 'There's none so blind as them that won't see,' he said. Annie wasn't sure what he meant by that.

He told her one of his hobgoblin stories, but she could think only of Screecher and the birds in the barn.

She wasn't at all surprised then to see Screecher fly into her dream. He flew in through the window and perched on the end of her bed. There was something in his beak. He let it fall on her bedcover. She sat up to get a closer look. It was a dead swallow.

'He's going to knock down the barn,' said Screecher.

'Who is?' said Annie.

'Your father. We heard him. Colly and me.'

'Colly?'

'That's Colly lying on your bed,' Screecher said. 'I tried to tell her, I told her she'd kill herself if she worked so hard. She never stopped – all day and every day. We've got to finish it, she said, and then they won't have to knock down our home.'

'Home?' said Annie.

'That barn is our home. We've got nowhere else to live. You've got to stop him. You've got to tell your father or else he'll bring in the bulldozer.'

'But he won't believe me,' said Annie. 'He doesn't believe anything I say. You tell him. He'll believe you, he'll listen to you.' And Screecher was suddenly gone.

It's a funny thing about dreams, they always seem to finish just as you wake up. There was a rumbling outside Annie's window, and voices. She sat up and looked out. Her father was standing by a great yellow bulldozer that belched black smoke and he was pointing up at the barn. Annie looked down and saw the swallow lying on her bed. She picked it up. Colly was limp in her hand, her beak half open. Annie never bothered with slippers or her dressing gown. She ran crying out of the house. Grandad heard her and her mother heard her. Her father heard nothing until the driver of the bulldozer switched off his engine and pointed at Annie as she came running up the path. Her father looked at the swallow in her hand.

'That's Colly isn't it?' he said.

Annie looked at him amazed. 'You know?' she said.

'I had a visitor last night,' he said. 'He told me everything, Annie. He brought me out here to show me the hole they'd mended. When I woke up this morning I thought I'd been sleepwalking, so I came and had another look. I wasn't dreaming, Annie.'

'Neither was I,' said Annie.

Grandad came puffing up the path, with mother behind him. 'What's going on?' said Grandad. 'What's that bulldozer for?'

'Oh nothing,' said Annie's father. 'Just took a wrong turning somewhere, that's all. Lost his way. We all do that from time to time, don't we Grandad?'

They buried Colly that morning in the corner of Long Meadow under the great ash tree. If Annie had looked up she'd have seen Screecher perched high above her, half hidden by the leaves, Colly's fledglings beside him. And they weren't alone. Every branch, every twig of the tree was lined with silent birds.

CONKER
CHAPTER ONE

MOST DOGS HAVE ONE NAME, BUT Pooch had three – one after the other. Pooch was what Grandma called him in the first place. But when Nick was a toddler he couldn't say Pooch very well and so Pooch soon became Pooh.

Then one day Pooh heard the rattle of the milk bottles outside and came bounding out of the house to say hello to the milkman – he liked the milkman. But today it was a different one. Pooh prowled around him sniffing at the bottom of his trousers. The new milkman went as white as his milk. Nick tried to drag Pooh back into the house, but he wouldn't come.

'S'like a wolf,' said the milkman, putting his hands on his head and backing down the path. 'You ought to chain it up.'

'Not a wolf,' Nick said. 'He's an old station.'

'A what?' said the milkman.

'An old station,' Nick said. 'Pooh is an old station.' At that moment Grandma came to the door.

'Nick gets his words muddled sometimes,' she said. 'He's only little. I think he means an *Alsatian*, don't you dear? Old station! Old station! You are a funny boy, Nick.' And she laughed so much that she nearly cried. So from that day Pooh was called Old Station.

There were always just the three of them in the house. Nick had lived with Grandma for as long as he could remember. She looked after Nick and Old Station looked after them both. Everywhere they went Old Station went with them. 'Don't know what we'd do without him,' Grandma would say.

All his life Old Station had been like a big brother to Nick. Nick was nine years old now. He had watched Old Station grow old as he grew up. The old dog moved slowly these days, and when he got up in the morning to go outside you could see it was a real effort. He would spend most of the day asleep in his basket, dreaming his dreams.

Nick watched him that morning as he ate his cornflakes before he went off to school. It was the last day before half-term. Old Station was growling in his sleep as he often did and his whiskers were twitching.

'He's chasing cats in his dreams,' said Grandma. 'Hurry up, Nick, else you'll be late.' She gave him his satchel and packed lunch, and Nick called out, 'Goodbye,' to Old Station and ran off down the road.

It was a windy autumn morning with the leaves falling all around him. Before he got to school he caught twenty-six of them in mid-air and that was more than he'd ever caught before. By the end of the day the leaves were piled as high as his ankles in the gutters, and Nick scuffled through them on the way back home, thinking of all the bike rides he could go on now that half-term had begun.

Old Station wasn't there to meet him at the

door as he sometimes was, and Grandma wasn't in the kitchen cooking tea as she usually was. Old Station wasn't in his basket either.

Nick found Grandma in the back garden, taking the washing off the line. 'Nice windy day. Wanted to leave the washing out as long as possible,' she said from behind a sheet. 'I'll get your tea in a minute, dear.'

'Where's Old Station?' Nick said. 'He's not in his basket.'

Grandma didn't reply, not at first anyway; and when she did Nick wished she never had done.

'He had to go,' Grandma said simply, and she walked past him without even looking at him.

'Go where?' Nick asked. 'What do you mean? Where's he gone to?'

Grandma put the washing down on the kitchen table and sat down heavily in the chair. Nick could see then that she'd been crying, and he knew that Old Station was dead. 'The vet said he was suffering,' she said, looking up at him. 'We couldn't have him suffering, could we? It had to be done. That's all there is to it. Just a pinprick it was, dear, and then he went off to sleep. Nice and peaceful.'

'He's dead then,' Nick said.

Grandma nodded. 'I buried him outside in the garden by the wall. It's what was best for him, Nick,' she said. 'You know that, don't you?' Nick nodded and they cried quietly together.

After tea Grandma put Old Station's basket out in the shed and showed Nick where she had buried him. 'We'll plant something over him, shall we, dear?' she said. 'A rose perhaps, so we don't forget him.'

'We'll never forget him,' said Nick. 'Never.'

CHAPTER TWO

THE DAY AFTER OLD STATION DIED WAS Saturday. Saturdays and Sundays in the conker season meant conkers in Jubilee Park with his friends, but Nick didn't feel like seeing anyone, not that day. Every time he looked out of the kitchen window into the back garden he felt like crying. It was Grandma's idea that he should go for a long ride, and so he did. The next best thing in the world after Old Station was the bike Grandma had given him on his birthday. It was shining royal blue with three-speed gears, a bell, a front light and everything. Just to sit on it made him feel happy. By the time he got back from his ride he felt a lot better.

The next morning Nick went off to Jubilee Park as he always did on a Sunday. All his friends were there, and so was Stevie Rooster. Stevie Rooster called himself the Conker King of Jubilee Park. He was one of those bragging brutish boys who could hit harder, run faster and shout louder than anyone else. There was only one thing Stevie had ever been frightened of, and that was Old Station. Perhaps it was because of Old Station that Nick was the one boy he had never bullied.

Of course they all knew about Old Station, but no one said anything about him, except for Stevie Rooster. 'So that smelly old dog of yours kicked the bucket at last,' he said. Perhaps he was expecting everyone to laugh, but no one did.

Nick tried to stop himself from crying.

Stevie went on, ''Bout time if you ask me.'

In his fury Nick tore the conker out of Stevie Rooster's hand and hurled it into the pond.

'That's my twenty-fiver!' Stevie bellowed, and he lashed out at Nick with his fist, catching him in the mouth.

Nick looked at the blood on the back of his hand and flew at Stevie's throat like an alley cat. In the end Nick was left with a split lip, a black eye and a torn shirt. He was lucky to get away with just that. If the Park Keeper had not come along when he did it might have been a lot worse.

Grandma shook her head as she bathed his face in the kitchen. 'What does it matter what Stevie Rooster says about Old Station?' she said. 'Look what he's done to you. Look at your face.'

'I had to get him,' Nick said.

'But you didn't, did you? I mean he's bigger than you isn't he? He's twice your size and nasty with it. If you want to beat him, you've got to use your head. It's the only way.'

'What do you mean, Grandma?' Nick asked. 'What else could I do?'

'Conkers,' said Grandma. 'Didn't you tell me once that he likes to call himself the Conker King of Jubilee Park?'

'Yes.'

'Well then,' said Grandma. 'You've got to knock him off his throne, haven't you?'

'But how?'

'You've got to beat him at conkers,' she said. 'And I'm going to teach you how. There's nothing I don't know about conkers, Nick, nothing. You'll see.'

CHAPTER THREE

SOMEHOW NICK HAD NEVER THOUGHT OF his Grandma as a conker expert.

'First we must find the right conkers,' she went on. 'And there's only one place to find a champion conker and that's from the old conker tree out by Cotter's Yard. It's still standing, I saw it from the bus only the other day. I never had a conker off that tree that let me down. Always hard as nails they are. Mustn't be any bigger than my thumbnail. Small and hard is what we're after.'

And so it was that Nick found himself that

afternoon cycling along the road out of town, past the football ground and the gasworks, with a packet of jelly babies in his pocket. 'Now don't eat them all at once, dear,' Grandma had told him. 'Go carefully and look for the tree on the left-hand side of the road just as you come to Cotter's Yard; you know, the scrapyard where they crunch up old cars. You can't miss it.' And Grandma's conker tree was just where she said it was, a great towering conker tree standing on its own by the scrapyard.

Nick must have spent half an hour searching through the leaves under the tree, but he couldn't find a single conker. He was about to give up and go home when he spotted a cluster of prickly green balls lying in the long grass on the other side of the fence. There was no sign of life in Cotter's Yard. No one would be there on a Sunday afternoon. No one would mind if he went in just to pick up conkers. There was nothing wrong with that he thought.

He climbed quickly. At the top he swung his legs over and dropped down easily on the other side. He found the cluster of three small conkers and broke them open. Each one was shining brown and perfect, and just the right size. He stuffed them into his pocket and was just about to climb out again when he heard from somewhere behind him in Cotter's Yard, the distant howling of a dog. His first thought was to scramble up over the fence and escape, but then the howling stopped and the dog began to whine and whimper and yelp. It was a cry for help which Nick could not ignore.

Cotter's Yard was a maze of twisted rusting wrecks. The muddy tracks through it were littered with car tyres. Great piles of cars towered all about him now as he picked his way round the potholes. And all the while the pitiful howling echoed louder around him. He was getting closer.

He found the guard dog sitting by a hut in the centre of the yard. He was chained by the neck to a metal stake, and he was shivering so much that his teeth were rattling. The chain was twisted over his back and wrapped around his back legs so that he could not move. Doesn't look ferocious, Nick thought, but you never know. And he walked slowly around the guard dog at a safe distance.

And then Nick noticed the dog's face. It was as if Old Station had come back from the grave and was looking up at him. He had the same gentle brown eyes, the same way of holding his head on one side when he was thinking. Old Station liked jelly babies, Nick thought. Perhaps this one will. One by one the dog took them gently out of Nick's hand, chewed them, swallowed them and then waited for the next one. When there were no more Nick gave him the paper bag to play with whilst he freed him from the chain. He ate the bag too, and when he stood up and shook himself, Nick could see that he was thin like a greyhound is thin. There were sores around his neck behind his ears where his collar had rubbed him raw.

Nick sat down beside him, took off his duffle coat and rubbed him and rubbed him until his teeth stopped chattering. He didn't like to leave him, but it was getting dark. 'Don't worry,'

Nick said, walking away. The dog followed him
to the end of his chain. 'I'll be back,' he said. 'I
promise I will.' Nick knew now exactly what
he wanted to do, but he had no idea at all how
he was going to do it.

It was dark by the time Nick got home and Grandma was not pleased with him. 'Where have you been? I was worried sick about you,' she said, taking off his coat and shaking it out.

'The conkers were difficult to find, Grandma,' Nick said, but he said no more.

Grandma was pleased with the conkers though. 'Just like they always were,' she said, turning them over in her hands. 'Unbreakable little beauties.' And then Grandma began what she called her conker magic. First she put them in the oven for exactly twelve minutes. Then she took them out and dropped them still hot into a pudding basin full of her conker potion, a mixture of vinegar, salt, mustard and a teaspoon of Worcester Sauce. One hour later she took them out again and put them back into the oven for another twelve minutes. When they came out they were dull and crinkled. She polished them with furniture polish till they shone again. Then she drove a small brass nail through the conkers one after the other and examined each one carefully. She put two of them aside and held up the third in triumph.

'This is the one,' she said. 'This is your champion conker. All you have to do now, Nick, is sleep with that down the bottom of your bed tonight and tomorrow. you'll be Conker King of Jubilee Park.'

But Nick couldn't sleep that night. He lay there thinking of the dog he had left behind in Cotter's Yard, and about how he was going to rescue him. By breakfast the next morning he was still not sure how to set about it.

'Remember, you must play on a short string,' Grandma was saying. 'And always play on grass so it won't break if he pulls it out of your hand. And try not to get tangled up – puts a strain on the knot. What's the matter with you, dear? You're not eating your breakfast.'

'Grandma,' Nick said, 'what if you found a dog all chained up and lonely and miserable, would you try to rescue it?'

'What makes you ask a thing like that, dear?' Grandma said.

'Would you?' Nick asked.

'Of course, dear.'

'Even if it meant stealing it, Grandma?'

'Ah well, that's different. Two wrongs

don't make a right, Nick,' she said. 'What's all this about?'

'Oh nothing, nothing,' Nick said quickly. 'I was just thinking, that's all.' Nick could feel she was suspicious. He had said far too much already. He left quickly before she could ask any more questions.

'Good luck, Nick,' Grandma called after him as he went off down the path.

He cycled right up to Stevie Rooster in the Park and challenged him there and then. 'I've got a conker that'll beat any conker you've got,' he said. Stevie Rooster laughed at Nick and his little conker, but when his first conker broke in two the smile left his face. He took conker after conker out of his sack, and each one was shattered into little pieces within seconds. A crowd gathered as Nick's conker became a twentier, a thirtier, a fiftier and then at last an eighty-fiver. Stevie Rooster's face was red with fury as he took his last conker out of his sack.

'Your turn,' Nick said quietly and he held up his conker. There still wasn't a mark on it. Stevie swung again and was left holding a piece of empty string with a knot swinging at the end of it. Nick looked him in the face and saw the tears of humiliation start into his eyes. 'You shouldn't have said that about Old Station,' Nick said and he turned, got on his bike and cycled off leaving a stunned crowd behind him.

CHAPTER FOUR

IT WAS A TWENTY MINUTE RIDE UP TO Cotter's Yard, but Nick did it in ten. All through the conker game he had been thinking about it and now at last he knew what to do. He had a plan. He was breathless by the time he got there. The gates were wide open. The yard was working today, the great crane swinging out over the crushing machine, a car hanging from its jaws.

'Hey you, what're you after?' It was a voice from the door of the hut. It belonged to a weasel-faced man with mean little eyes.

'I've come to buy your dog,' Nick said.

'Haven't got any money, but I'll swop my bike for your dog. It's almost new, three speed and everything. Had it for my birthday, a month ago.' Nick looked around for the dog, but there was no sign of him. The chain lay curled up in the mud by the hut.

'Haven't got no dog here,' said the weasel-faced man, 'not any more. Wasn't any use anyway. Got rid of him, didn't I?'

'What do you mean?' Nick said.

'Just what I said. I got rid of him. Vet came and took him away this morning. No use to me he wasn't. Now push off out of here.' And he went back inside the hut and slammed the door behind him.

As Nick walked home, the rain came spitting down through the trees. He had never felt more miserable in his life. When Old Station had died he had been sad enough, but this was different and much, much worse. This had been his fault. If only he had come back earlier, if only. By the time he reached home he was blinded with tears.

'Well, and how's the Conker King of Jubilee Park?' Grandma called out from the kitchen as he closed the door behind him, and she came hurrying out to meet him. 'Well I told you, didn't I? I told you. It's all down the street. Everyone knows my Nick's the Conker King. Well, come on, let's see the famous conker. An eighty-fiver, isn't it?'

'Eighty-sixer,' Nick said and burst into tears against her apron.

'What's all this?' Grandma said, putting an arm round him and leading him into the kitchen. 'We can't have the Conker King of Jubilee Park crying his eyes out.' And Nick blurted it all out, all about Cotter's Yard and the poor starving dog he had found there that looked just like Old Station, about how the vet had come and taken him away.

'I was going to buy him for you with my bike,' Nick said, 'to take Old Station's place, but I was too late.'

'Who says you were?' said Grandma, and there was a certain tone in her voice.

'What do you mean?' Nick asked.

'What I mean, dear, is that if you'd wipe your eyes and look over in the corner there, you'd see a basket with a dog in it, and if you looked hard at that dog you might just recognise him.'

Nick looked. The dog from Cotter's Yard lay curled up in Old Station's basket, his great brown eyes gazing up at him. The dog got up, stretched, yawned and came over to him.

'But how . . .?' Nick began.

Grandma held up her hand.

'When you came home from Cotter's Yard yesterday with your duffle coat stinking of dog, I was a little suspicious. You see, old Cotter's known for the cruel way he looks after his guard dogs, always has been. And then when you asked me this morning if I would rescue

a dog if I found him all chained up and hungry and miserable – well, I put two and two together.'

'But he said the vet came and took him away – he told me,' Nick said.

'So he did, dear, so he did. We went out there together, the vet and me, and we made old Cotter an offer he couldn't refuse. Either we took his dog with us or we reported him for cruelty to animals. Didn't take him long to make up his mind, I can tell you.'

'So he's ours then, Grandma?' Nick said.

'Yours, Nick, he's yours. Old Station was mine. I had him even before I had you, remember? But this one's yours, your prize for winning the Conker Championship of Jubilee Park. Now can I see that famous conker or can't I?'

Nick fished the conker out of his pocket and held it up by the string. Before he knew it, the dog had jumped up and jerked it out of his hand. A few seconds later all that was left was a mass of wet crumbs and chewed string.

'It looks as if he likes conkers for his tea,' Grandma said.

'Better call him Conker then,' Nick said. And so they did.